Martin Luther King Jr. Day

For Jayden Smith
—M. M.

ISBN-13: 978-0-545-10433-3
ISBN-10: 0-545-10433-5

Text copyright © 2007 by Brenda Bowen.
Illustrations copyright © 2007 by Mike Gordon.
All rights reserved. Published by Scholastic Inc., 557 Broadway, New York, NY 10012, by arrangement with Simon & Schuster Books for Young Readers, an imprint of Simon & Schuster Children's Publishing Division. READY-TO-READ is a registered trademark of Simon & Schuster, Inc. SCHOLASTIC and associated logos are trademarks and/or registered trademarks of Scholastic Inc.

12 11 10 9 8 7 6 5 4 3 2   9 10 11 12 13 14/0

Printed in the U.S.A.   23

First Scholastic printing, January 2009

Designed by Sammy Yuen Jr.

The text of this book was set in Century Schoolbook BT.

Martin Luther King Jr. Day

Written by Margaret McNamara
Illustrated by Mike Gordon

Ready-to-Read

SCHOLASTIC INC.
New York Toronto London Auckland Sydney
Mexico City New Delhi Hong Kong Buenos Aires

One day in January, Mrs. Connor took the first graders to a museum.

"Does anyone know
who this is?" she asked.

Ayanna knew the answer.
"That is the Reverend Doctor
Martin Luther King Junior,"
said Ayanna.

Mrs. Connor said,
"Doctor King was a
great leader because he
had great dreams."

"What kind of dreams?"
asked Reza.

"They were very big dreams,"
said Mrs. Connor,
"about how to make the
world a better place."

Back at school, Mrs. Connor asked the class to draw their dreams on a piece of paper.

They had big dreams,
just like Doctor King.

"I have a dream that there
will be no more fighting,"
Eigen said.

"I have a dream that the
earth will be clean,"
said Hannah.

"I have a dream that
everyone will have fun,"
Katie said.

"I have a dream that people
will never get sick!"
Nia said.

"I have a dream that I will do good things," said Becky.

"I have a dream that all children will play together," Emma said.

"I have a dream that no one will be poor," said James.

25

"I have a dream that everyone will be safe," Reza said.

The first graders were happy
with their dreams.

"Doctor King would be proud
of you," said Mrs. Connor.

"What is your dream?"
Ayanna asked Mrs. Connor.

"Oh, I have a very big dream,"
said Mrs. Connor.

"I have a dream,"
said Mrs. Connor,
"that all your dreams
will come true."